All this and a Bag of Chips

Mary-Ellen & Richard DiPietra

DEDICATION

To
Nick Ray
We love you bigger than the sky

CONTENTS

Seashell
Sara Rude
Emerson
Tribute
Self on a shelf

You can call me Joe

My name is Richard Joseph DiPietra.
Joseph was my confirmation name. Di Pietra
means 'of rock' in Italian. I go by Richard

I've been called: Ricardo, Rich, Richie,
Sailor, Guppy, Gup.

And there was this beautiful hippie chick
Jan, who wore thick mod glasses in the 70's
who called me Joe. When I corrected her, she
smiled and said, ``everyone is Joe to me."
Good enough.

These are some of my stories. Hope you
enjoy.

Our first book, I am a Cuban Sandwich was

centered around Ybor City and the great food
you found there. Since this is sort of a side
dish of stories, we thought we would start out
with candy. Please eat with a fork, spoon and
open heart!

Joes' Grocery

Nebraska Avenue, Joe's grocery, that's
where everybody bought candy. Joe was the
one that taught me to make kites.

I loved Zero bars! They were the best!.
They would even freeze them sometimes. It
had a polar bear on top, still my favorite
animal. It was mostly nought, nuts inside, big
good sized nuts! A good candy bar.

To drink I would always get a root beer,
could be Hyers or Hoffman's...like the song...
    'The prettiest girl I ever saw, was sipping
Hoffman's right through a straw....'

The Boss

The boss has not been happy. He's been getting complaints from his neighbors and that ain't good no way no how. He likes for everything to go smoothly and when it doesn't, well, you get the picture.

He's got us out at his country property, keeping an eye on everything. Tonight we're out in the middle of nowhere. It's black as a crow out there.

But something just don't seem right. We're hearing low noises, seems like something's out there. What it is, I got no idea, so me and the guys, we're checking things out to see what might be going on that we don't know about.

The boss has brought in an old friend of his from his days in the army. A Purple Heart winner, Bobbie knows his way around in any situation. He's been keeping an eye on everything just in case.

All of a sudden there's a big commotion. Guys are yelling and raising hell. The boss grabs one of his guys and tells him, "That noise is coming from over near the creek. Head over there and check it out.

Take the sawed off just in case."

So we're out in front of the cabin, the noise getting near and we see Bobbie lighting up a smoke and I tell him, "Bob, what the hell is going on?"

He tells me it's coming from over there near those big oaks.

"What we got, cops?"

"No," he says, cool as a cucumber

"Feds?" I ask.

"Unh, unh."

"What then?"

He flashes this big ass grin and says, "Cows! We got about 20 head of cows down there!"

Well, we're laughing our asses off when the boss comes up all pissed off. "What the hell are you assholes laughing at?"

We tell him and he starts laughing his ass off too. "Bedda matri! I almost opened up on a herd of cows! I wouldn't have been able to show my face for a whole year if I pulled a bone head move like that. They woulda been calling me Rawhide! And Singing Rolli'n,Rollin' w

when I walked down the street! I never woulda lived that down!

Chicken in a Bag

My name is Mocobrain, and I grew up in Ybor City, Florida. Well, my name is really Thomas after some saint, but no one ever called me that. There were eight kids in our family, everyone had a nickname. I think my father didn't even know half of our real birth certificate names. My dad used to deliver milk for the Florida Dairy. Sometimes on a heavy day, me and my brothers would ride along with him to help out. Over the years, I was familiar with everyone in the area ...mostly hard-working folks that didn't have

a lot of money. I never had much money
myself. There were so many kids in our
family, good Catholics, poor providers. I once
saw my mother share a single can of tuna for
the entire eight of us. How did she do that?

But it always seemed some other guys in
the neighborhood had everything they
needed and wanted all the time. Their dads
had jobs that let them hang around all the
time, and yet their kids always had the green.
I just didn't get it.

Eventually this led to trying to find ways to
make some money of my own. I got a job with
one of the smaller grocery stores as a bagboy.
I was young and stupid ... I thought I hung
around with a dangerous crowd. It was tough
seeing the managers and owners flashing big
rolls around while I had very little in my
pocket. This led me to think up ways to get
some of this money myself. I spent as much
time as I could poking around in the back
room and always tried to get a look at the
boss when there was money being counted or
exchanged. Little by little, I formulated a plan
and began to work at accomplishing my goal.
I began to take a lot of interest in how money
was moved around or saved. Makes sense,
right? It was better to make my play when the
money was more available, so I asked for

more night shifts, and I kept my eye on how and when any money was passed.

Finally, I got my chance. Saturday was the biggest money day, so I planned for that. I had talked it up to some of my pals in the backroom that were ready to make the play late on Friday night. It all took place in the back storage room/freezer area of the store. It was pretty dark and scary back there.

There were some guys from the local farm bringing in fresh poultry in grocery bags and some smart guys stuffing bags with cash. It all went down just like we hoped it would. I grabbed one of the bags and bolted out the back door. I stuffed it in my backpack and took off like a madman. I didn't see anybody else around so I ran without stopping up to Dale Mabry and I jumped on the first bus that stopped. I made my way to the back of the bus and slid down to hide myself. We were heading for I - 4 which worked out perfect. I 'd be gone before anybody had a clue.

We cruised past a few blocks, and looking around I didn't see anyone following or hear any sirens. I had the grocery bag and nobody was looking for me as far as I could tell. I was feeling pretty darn good about everything. I saw another bus pull up to a stop, so I grabbed my bag of knapsack of cash and bolted out the door. I got on the second bus and made my way down the aisle to the back, hugging the bag as I saw cops cruising by with their lights on. I slid down in my seat, craning my neck around and keeping an eye on everything. The sirens were heading the other way. I breathed a big sigh of relief and put the bag of cash on my lap almost hugging it. It was only then that I noticed how heavy the bag was. And cold. I looked in it and saw that like a fool, I had grabbed the wrong bag and in my lap was a big frozen chicken. I guess the nickname makes a little more sense now, huh?

Gidget's not gone

I read today, Sandra Dee, who shot to fame as the sweet and lovable teen surfer in the movie Gidget, died at 62. We never know what is really going to test us; what will mash those buttons and make us catch a quick breath. So as a middle-aged man who made it through the 50's, 60's and 70's, I was completely unprepared for the blow.

The vision of Sandra Dee's light blonde hair bouncing in a ponytail will always be etched in my mind. Her storybook romance and wedding to teen heartthrob Bobby Darin sadly did not last long and after that her career was pretty much over, it barely lasted 10 years. She battled a host of ills most of her life. I can remember seeing a picture of her in an old Photoplay magazine of my moms; at a party having fun but smoking a cigarette. Everybody disapproved, refusing to let her grow up. Tragically, it was the smoking that shortened her life.

But Gidget, on the other hand, was irrepressible and intelligent with a passion and determination for living her life. She was so young, innocent, unsure and self-conscious, hey wait a minute, so was I! Gidget epitomized it for us all, although most are not probably willing to admit it. Just think about it; a teenager from California, spends a lot of time at the beach, learns to surf becoming one of the first girls to get off the beach and onto the board. In doing so, she falls in love for the first time and comes into her own, outpacing all those

13

around her - cool surfers and parents alike.

And this was 1959, people, that's before the Beatles, much less the Beach Boys, who I would bet coughed up some of their allowance to go see Gidget, at least once, and were certainly as inspired by her as the ultra-hip surfers they wrote songs about.

I only glanced at the photos of Sandra Dee's life, content to favor my own images but my eyes stung, nonetheless, and the loss of such a lovely young star that burned out like a comet, rattled me deeply. I went outside. I needed more air, more time, more hope.

So, I go down to the beach. A little cool and breezy here at Upham Beach, almost like a California day, and there is even a modest smooth curl. Just a handful of surfers are out, making the best of what they can get from the area beach.

I fight off another wave of nostalgia and sadness and then...there she is...Gidget! A small group of surfers have come on shore and one is a young girl in a full wetsuit. Her hair is darker and her board is certainly smaller, but she is so small and lively, it's almost unsettling. Instead, I prefer to feel reassured. Yeah, it goes on. Anyway, I muse as I head back to the car, that's not Gidget. Gidget is at home waiting for me to have sandwiches and ice tea for lunch...really....she is, she just called me on my cell phone and told me she was taking off from work and would be right home!

Richard "Moondoggie" DiPietra

The Electric Zoo

1969... If you were to look down from an airplane bound for the Northeast corridor of the United

States, you might be able to make out a long

multi-colored line, snaking its way through the greenery, weaving in and out, on its way to the great Sunshine state of Florida.. And if you looked really carefully and happened to have a decent pair of binoculars , you might even notice the movement of vehicles of different types, small and large. But as you got closer to land, it would soon become clear that most of the movement was actually just that of people, making their way south. Apparently involved in some sort of migration or other. It Would soon become

clear to anyone with a sharp eye. of the reason for this. It all started in NYC over the Labor day weekend With the Electric Zoo on Randall's Island with people from all over, DJ's and live acts from different countries. In 1969, we were lucky to have The Allman Brothers Band, Who had performed several times in the ST Pete area. Bring their unique presence and atmosphere to

our bay area.

The word had got around that The

Brothers were sponsoring a Bikini contest and it was all

gonna be happening down by the river, ironic.Huh. Down here in Florida, we're all pretty used to most of these things but this was really looking like it was gonna be epic. I was happy to be in town to hook up with a friend from the old days. Been way too long and she was having some trouble. Looks like she could really use a break. The weather was warm but awesome and girls were showing off their assets left and right.

The river was cool and comfortable,people were cannonballing and rope swinging all over. And, It wasn't long before the bikinis started coming off! FLA Ya gotta love it!

Later on, we were hanging out at the club which was situated right in the middle of an old cemetery but there was a dance hall with music inside where the bands played. I was walking around checking things out on the floor, it was jamming and the band music was great. Then, out of nowhere, I thought I saw her. We had been tight for a while . It was sweet being with her.

Then, just like that she was gone. Or had I even seen her? And this ain't that big a town, know what I'm' sayin?

I asked around, nobody had seen her or knew anything. Then out of nowhere, the same club, she appears. I couldn't believe my eyes. I was nervously glancing over at her, then avoiding her eyes hoping to catch a glimpse. She was as sweet as I remembered,but now a young girl on the verge of womanhood. Finally as she was pouring drinks she caught me looking at her and with a small shy smile said, Yeah", it's me. I heard you had some trouble, I quietly asked her. She nodded her head towards the door. Turns out She got caught carrying. Luckily her father pulled some strings and got her probation. Six months is not too bad. We had a lotta catching up to do.Just then somebody burst in the

door and yelled, Hey! The Allman Brothers

are outside hitting the road! We headed
outside and watched them roar off into The
jet black Florida night. So cool I was getting a
James Dean vibe! Awesome!

ME
What's your name, little girl?

I was born on July 16. the feast of our Lady of Carmel. My mother told the story that she had been in labor for almost 48 hours when my uncle Jack and his Maryknoll seminarian buddy Fr. Jim Defino arrived at her bedside. They said she had to name me after the saint's day. Wanting them to go away she said yes. They named me Mary Carmela. My Aunt Mary says she was livid when she got home.

So I am Mary Carmela on my Baptisimal certificate. Cissy, my mum, officially changed it so, I am Mary-Ellen on my birth certificate.

Seemed to set me off at an odd pace.

I tended to wander, even as a child, and once my mother heard herself called over the loudspeaker at Alexanders on Fordham Road, "Will the parents of little Mary-Ellen come to the customer service desk." My mom always seemed a little peeved when she told this tale of me, because little me was found swinging my tiny legs and eating candy and ignoring her worry.

I go by Mary-Ellen. I just discovered the hyphen recently while examining the details of my birth certificate for some explanations. I noticed that my mom had put a hyphen in my name. Who knew? It's like a gift from her to me post mortality. Most online forms do not accept it, anyone who does not know me still calls me Mary, but this silly little punctuation mark makes me incredibly happy!

aka
MiMi/MoiMoi/Madre
Mellon
Mares
Mz Ellen
ME (pronounced EmEee)

CANDY

Saturday morning for me as a kid would start out trudging up the hill of Grand Avenue towards Fordham Road to John and Mary's corner store. For $1.00, I could furnish my entire weekend with fun. 25 would buy an Archie comic book double issue. 15 cents would buy a 'pinky', the pink spalding rubber ball that we would play with until it ended up down a sewer drain with it's millions of comrades. 12 cents would purchase six pieces of bazooka joe bubble gum. That offered candy and a comic! I always purchased for the group having learned never to blow bubbles solo. If you ever had to peel bubble gum out of your eyebrows you will understand.

Finally, the white bag o candy! Into this would go a sheet of the sugar buttons on paper, candy cigarettes, little wax soda bottles filled with sugar liquid, one or two mary janes, they took a while, and a sugar daddy, for later.

This treasure trove I would bring back to the front of my building, 'the stoop' and I would sit with my pink polka dotted box of 45s, portable pink record player/radio, comic books and candy. All day long. kids from the block would come by, chew gum, share their comic books, and play handball against the stoop and stick ball between the parked cars in the street. We would bounce the ball in front of us and under one leg to rhymes, "A my name is Alice and my husband's name is Alan. We live in Alaska and we eat apples."

I know now that living in an ancient five story walk up building meant we were poor. I didn't know that then. Those Saturdays, I was the Queen of the Bronx!

High Heels

"Lady, get your head out of the clouds and move that car!" The irate cab driver was a welcome distraction from my emotional state when I dropped my parents off at Kennedy Airport. It wasn't my head that was the problem; it was my heart. A palpable feeling, so real to me that the thought crossed my mind that this heartache was actually

23

causing me to gain weight. Just what I needed, two months before my wedding.

Through the revolving doors from the steamy outside and the air conditioning hits you like a welcome slap. As I spied them waiting at the Aer Lingus line, my parents' opposing attitude had that same effect on me. Talk about role reversal. As distressed as I was, you could see how happy they were. In their Sunday best, they were already chatting up everyone online. Ellen and Peter Loonam were, Cis and Pete to anyone who knew them. My mom was called Cissy. She was like a sister to the world, someone anyone could talk to and someone who would listen.

My father was excited to be going Home to Ireland, home with a capital H. After 25 years in New York, a small town in the middle of another island world still drew him. Cissy was just as thrilled, she loved all things Irish with a passion that even the Irishborn recognized and respected.

I had grown up with the culture and

history of the People along with mother's milk, a world away in the Bronx. Now just watching my mother move along, even sitting in a wheelchair, she was a bundle of energy and motion but I just held my breath and waited because I knew she was fighting so much pain wearing a full length cast, ankle to hip, to support the knee that was riddled with cancer. She had beat cancer before. We had been through it together. Many times.

I was four, when she was diagnosed the first time, back in the 50's, they sent her to what was called at the time, 'Death Therapy' to help her accept her situation. My grandmother told me the story of when my mom came home for the first time from this therapy. That night I was put to bed early. My mother said she could not face the battle of illness ahead and was going up to the roof to end it all. My grandmother was shocked when my Dad said, "Ok, I'll go with you." They walked up together onto Tar Beach, the roof, and had one last cigarette under the stars to calm her nerves. This was the 50's after all. There was a tearful goodbye, one more last cigarette, one last kiss and then my Dad said, "Oh, by the way, what do you want me to tell that little girl downstairs?" My mom shouted her curses at him and the night sky, they came back downstairs and she never looked back. From that moment on, she faced every illness as a personal challenge. "I can beat this," she said, over and over again. "Pray." And we did.

Watching their plane take off heading out over the ocean, leaving me alone, was tough. But, I knew that for my mom and dad, being in their special place would weave its magic on them and I also knew my mother was perhaps saying goodbye to the place and people she held dearest.

The radiation pellet that they had inserted into the tumor on her knee, a brand new, hopeful treatment, had failed to stop the spread of the disease this time. After prognosis, Cis had talked them into letting her take this trip. They wanted her to stay and continue treatment and monitoring. She had been through so much, for so long, her poor heart was worn down and had suffered several cardiac episodes. Unfortunately, those caregivers were just using numbers to evaluate her condition. They had no idea of the strength of her lion-sized heart. I did. I had been her cub and by now had, personally, seen her defeat death several times. And they also were not counting on my Dad. The love of her life, who would do anything, no matter what it took. If the boats and planes were down, he would have built her a nice wooden bridge across the Atlantic Ocean.

Now, on their return from the Emerald Isle, the "powers that be" wanted to amputate her leg. She had recovered from her mastectomy ten years ago, like the trooper she always was. She joked that now she had a reason to buy fancy new bras. I knew she had the courage; it just felt like her poor body would not have the strength.

In spite of the six hour time difference, they called me that night to say they had arrived safely. I could hear the music and laughter behind them. I could hear the joy in my mother's voice, she was Home! But as I hung up the phone, all I could feel was fear.

I was working on Wall Street and every afternoon during lunch, I would go to the Adam and Eve chapel, an amazing space of solitude and quiet in the very heart of one of the busiest streets in the entire world. The few other souls who wandered in, seemed to always respect the sacred silence. Motes of dust glistened in the air as sunlight streamed through the glorious stained glass windows. Every day, I went and prayed. I would say my rosary, praying to the Blessed Mother. She was a mother herself, so she would help protect mine.

Yet, out of the peace and quiet, the questions would come. Why now, I kept asking? Now, just when I had met the man I loved and was starting my own life. The landmarks in my life had always been like punctuation points in the handling of her illnesses. She would say, "I will make it until your Communion", as she recovered from colon cancer. "Until, you finish high school", as she beat uterine cancer. When she made it to my college graduation, the first woman in our family, I was as proud of her, as I was of myself, she had survived!

Since there was a six hour time difference, we would set up times for my parents to call me. Each night, I would wait anxiously by the phone. My fiancée was surprised by my anxiety. He knew all the positives we had all been through and talked about as a family, so, what was different now? I couldn't understand my feelings either, it made me short tempered and confused.

Over the phone, my mother was full of stories about the relatives they were seeing in all the places they visited. They went to Clonmacnoise, one of our favorite places and prayed. We got choked up on both sides of the ocean. If any prayers would work, we knew it would be from such a beloved and sacred place.

On the phone, my Dad tried to lighten things up telling me about a Clontarf monastery they had just gotten permission to visit. A cousin who was a priest had arranged an invitation to a very reclusive order of monks. It was said they held a relic of Padre Pio, who had just died.

If someone who is devoted to a religious figure could be called a fan, my mom was a fan of the beloved Padre. Even more than his miracles, his stigmata and suffering resonated with her as she battled cancer. Dad chatted a bit about the history then rang off, saying the next time we talked, they would be back in New York.

My fiancé, Richard accompanied me to their return. Knowing how emotional I felt, he was being even more thoughtful and considerate than usual. As I stood there, scanning the crowd of arrivals at Customs, he gave me a hug and said he would be right back. I was so grateful to have found a man that revered his family and mine as well. After what seemed like forever, he returned with chocolate for me and flowers for my mom. A lifetime later, I can still remember how touched I was by that small gesture. "Violets," he said, "her favorite".

The first people to get to the baggage carousel for their flight, I was practically jumping up and down with excitement. I had missed them both so much. Then, I saw my father come around the corner from Customs. I didn't see the wheelchair with my mother and had a moment of panic but, then there she was standing behind him with her hand on his shoulder. Wait, standing? I shook my head in disbelief, mouth completely dry, I could hardly swallow. I lowered my gaze to her feet and...she was wearing high heels. My mother had left America in a wheelchair with an amputation scheduled and now was standing in front of me in high heels!

Then, I had that experience I had seen portrayed in cartoons all my life. A circle of little white lights were floating around my head and everything went black. I fainted. Richard caught me and sat me down on a

nearby bench. As my head cleared, both my
parents were sitting on either side of me,
patting my back and looking concerned. A
cool drink revived me and on the ride to their
home upstate, I got the long explanation.

The monastery at Clontarf had indeed been
very old and very beautiful but what
happened inside was truly astonishing. They
were invited into a private room, where an
old priest, older than God himself, my dad
would say, kindly greeted them, asked a few
questions, and listened to their story. Then
sat and prayed with them before going to an
ornate chest. Opening it, he took out an
antique cloth telling them that contained in
the cloth was an actual chip of the bone of
Padre Pio who although not yet proclaimed a
Catholic saint was well known for his cures
and miracles.

Reverently taking the cloth, he rubbed it
along my mother's leg; next he held it to her
forehead and prayed. My mother would later
tell of the cold burning sensation she felt
from the touch of the holy cloth.

My Dad received his blessing as well and said he experienced the same strange sensation which gave him a feeling of great joy.

The next day, when she woke up, all the pain in her leg was gone. Later, back in the States, the doctors confirmed it, the tumor was gone! They had no explanation.

My mother never had cancer again. She lived a happy life to 80 years young. Richard and I married at my parents' beautiful lakeside home, surrounded by friends and family. My mother was the perfect hostess and even led the band in singing Irish rebel songs late into the night. She and my Dad retired to that same small town in Ireland, Banagher on the Shannon. No more trips to the airport were needed, because they were Home.

In His Arms

Their first night together, he woke from the soundest sleep he had ever known, limbs completely entangled up with hers. One shapely leg snaked between his muscular hairy ones. Her arms completely around him and his around her. He could not believe he had slept in that position. How had his limbs not gone numb? He breathed her scent, the smell of their lovemaking mingling with something between cucumber and roses. Wow, he thought, one night with her and I'm a poet. She stirred and sighed, nestling closer to him. He gently reclaimed his arms, moving hers from his waist. She smiled when he swiftly replaced himself with the pillow, she did this snuggle thing and seemed to drift back to sleep. He watched. She wasn't beautiful like the women he usually dated but he had to

34

admit she was lovely. So innocent and sweet, like a small child in her dreaming. Then she did the most amazing thing. She laughed. He couldn't believe it, it was such a surprising sound. Not the impish chuckle or the deep-throated laughter he would grow to adore later on but a musical, crescendo of ascending single notes of amusement. He had slept with many women, and had never heard any of them laugh in their sleep. He decided right then that he wanted to be the one to make her dreams so delightful.

In bed last night, as well, she had not been like any of the women he had known. Girlish. Although fit, she seemed delicate and he had felt protective of her. But after hours of kissing, when they finally decided to shed their clothes like old skins, she was passion purifying itself. She seemed to take delight in every touch, so deeply, he felt superfluous at times.

35

On top, they joined, as she rode him, she caressed her own breasts. This was all done with such frenzy and pleasure, he had a fleeting thought that she must have once been a man, she seemed to savor her female body, and take her own pleasure so directly. Later she proved that she cared very much about his pleasure. Now in the morning he retasted that memory and felt such gratitude that he wanted to wake her up and thank her and felt foolish for the impulse.

He had been with many women, some so beautiful, they took his breath away. Now it occurred to him that was all they had to offer. This loving gift of a perfect breast. If they wiggle their hips at all during the act, it was largely due to impatience. More aroused by the car he drove than his hand on their thigh. Not so, at all with Josette. She was a sexual musical instrument and he felt, for the first time ever... a virtuoso.

"Don't tell me it's morning already!" She moaned from beneath the pillow. Another dimension to this delightful creature. Grumpy in the morning. Ah ha! She is not perfect. He rejoiced, for He was the opposite. Once up, he was whistling and making his morning smoothie. This seemed to annoy her, so he quickly learned that a hot sweet beverage, coffee, tea, even hot water with lemon and honey, would bring himself and the rest of humanity back into the rosy glowing place that was her world.

And then he felt it, a split second of panic that he was, unfortunately going to experience over and over his lifelong. "What if I had not met her? What if I had not stayed late or missed that train? Had gone to pick up that wallet the day before like I was supposed to and I never saw her there, never crossed her crazy picket line?" This thought, even on that morning

37

after their first night together, made
his mouth go dry and his throat close.
He didn't even know if he would ever
see her again, but the alarm
overwhelmed him. Then she pulled on
his tee shirt and grinned as she
modeled it for him, pulling it tight to
accent her breasts, modest and sexy at
the same time, mocking herself and he
could swallow again and laugh with
her. It was the tiniest moment, but it
left him a little bit lightheaded. They
spent all the next day Saturday
together, wandering around the city,
and Saturday night and then Sunday,
and then the rest of their lives.

It was only the day before that
he had met her. In the doorway to one
of his favorite stores in New York,
McNally's. Since 1893, this red brick
building has been on 9th Avenue.
showcased a phantasmagorical
collection. A taxidermist's dream; a
full- sized peacock with tail fully

extended, large steamer trunks of teak or mahogany stickered by world travels proving their provenance from Paris to Hong Kong.

Rick had found this unique wallet for his father's birthday. It was made from rough cowhide with the hair still on it. He was having it engraved and had planned on picking it up yesterday so he could get it in the mail to Tampa. But his boss had decided this was the day to be everybody's buddy and pay for lunch. Not one to hang out with the office gang, somehow he got volunteered as a delivery man. And, that was why he was on his hurried way today.

A young woman holding a little white paper bag taped to a Popsicle stick bearing the words. THE MUFF'S ARE MINKS stood barring his way. Rick noticed her message had been scrawled with purple lipstick. As he approached, she pushed her scarf down and barked "Don't cross my picket line! Don't shop in this terrible place. They use living, well recently, live minks to make muffs." Tears pouring down her cheeks and taken by her ardor Rick moved to take out his handkerchief. Standing up straight with her hand squeezing his arm for emphasis, she continued "I just wanted to buy my Mom a muff like she had when she was a little girl. The sales lady showed me one with the face and paws of a tiny animal. I was admiring how real it looked when she told me that it looked real because it was real! That mink muff in my hand had been a live animal in Russia less than six months ago. I dropped it on the floor and ran, she yelled at me that this was a $800 muff and if I was not buying it I should not mishandle it. I ran out here and once I could get a grip, I decided to protest."

"I understand," He said in his most reasonable voice. Later she would say she didn't like him at first because of that placating tone. "But I am also purchasing a gift for a parent and I have already paid for it and had it engraved." She put her head down and seemed to think about it. "Well", she said as she let go of his arm, "I guess if it's engraved. But tell them how evil that is; the killing of little animals for their skin." He looked down at her long legs encased in high brown leather boots, admired them, then remarked. "Your boots are animal skin..." again in his most agreeable tone. "Yes, but they were not alive when they took their skin." She stopped, her face twisted in concern, "Are they?" His heart twisted at her expression and he immediately reassured her no, not at all. Her relief was palpable and with that small victory, he crossed her invisible picket line and went inside to pick up his purchase. He noticed she was not there when he left.

The afternoon's work poured in at its usual frantic pace. As he finished one turnaround report another appeared in his IN box. By 6:00, he was still not finished, but he was done. Donning his layers of winter armor, hat, coat, scarf, gloves, he headed for the subway. He reached the platform just as the express was closing its doors. People blocked the sliding doors with their bodies. He is barely able to slide in, ignoring the dirty looks of the folks who had just squeezed in seconds before. He angled himself until he got to his preferred spot, the last center holding bar near the end car. He closed his eyes for a second and as the sounds of clashing wheels on the tracks wash over him, he nods. Startled awake, he had to shake his head twice because he couldn't believe what he was seeing. A pretty young girl, at least he thought she might be pretty under that ridiculous hat and all those scarfs and sweaters, was actually getting up to offer an old man her seat. He had not seen that done lately. Bouncing around a bit as the train lurched, she moved over to grab onto the bar right next to his. She looked vaguely familiar, but he could not place her right away.

Rick was a complete failure as a cad. He adored women in general and was usually confused and offended by the casual callousness women and other men used to handle their relationships. He was afraid he was a bit of a romantic. He hoped this was not someone he had encountered and forgotten. Then it flashed on him.

That was that crazy girl from today at McMillians. The one with the purple lipstick sign!

Just then she spotted him. She waved and moved over to hold on to his same hanging pole. "Nice to see you

All This and A Bag of Chips

again." as if they had just met earlier at tea. "How did your engraving turn out"? What the hell is she talking about? What engraving? Was she talking about putting initials on minks? Obviously a total loon and a must to avoid. Gauging his expression, she sweetly offered, "Your Dad's wallet?" Finally realizing what she meant, he laughed deeply at himself. She was quick to join in and they both wound up laughing so hard that hardened New Yorkers near them even smiled a bit.

Suddenly, the lights went out. Though this is an everyday occurrence on the subway, she startled like a child and stepped a little closer to him. He felt a surge of confidence and took a step closer to her, shielding her with his own height from the mass of humanity, pressing around them. The train jerked forward a few times, before rolling backward to a standstill.

In the complete darkness and sudden silence, she reached for his hand. He leaned in close as she began to talk to him in low intimate tones, having no idea what she was saying, he just hoped she would never stop. She smelled so nice, unusual; clean yet spicy.

They got off the train together, had dinner, went to bed and the rest is history. They were married less than six months later, together since their first night. They had two weddings, one for her huge Irish family in the Bronx and one for his huge Cuban/Italian family in Tampa.

She had five brothers, each one taller than the other. They all lived in an old brownstone building, owned by their parents, Bridget and Patrick. Josette was the only Irish person Rick had ever met before he came to NYC. One of things he loved most about New

York was how it was divided into enclaves of immigrants finding haven among their own kind. Little Italy, Chinatown, Little Germany. In the Maloney neighborhood, you could hear thick brogues right off the boat and smell corned beef and cabbage cooking in every hallway and alley shaft.

It was the same for Rick back in Florida. He was a Cuban Sandwich, where he came from in Ybor City, Spanish pork, Cuban ham and Italian salami all went into the classic sandwich. Just like they all went into Rick. Spanish grandparent, Cuban mother, Italian father. Nobody else ever laughed at that joke when he first moved to NY, no one had heard of that style sandwich at the time, until Josette. That's why he loved her. She didn't have to understand details, she just got him.

The   brothers   were   very

protective of their little sister and gave
Rick as hard a time as they could the
first few nights she brought him home.
After the wedding, when they knew for
sure how much he loved her and saw
how happy he made her, they accepted
him completely and treated him as a
brother. Best friends, Dearest
comrades. Rick never dreamed of such
richness of connections and
relationships. He had been an only
child; his parents were both college
professors and intellectuals, more
interested in classic subjects than their
own lives. Their holiday dinner was a
lively game of scrabble. Relatives were
seen only at church, holidays and
funerals.

Now he had real friends, as well
as family. She had opened him up to
new ways of caring for others he had
never even imagined. His intimacy
issues seemed to melt under the
warmth of their love, and he gratefully
embraced her world, instead of forcing

his colder, if not more organized world on her.

Football, baseball, hockey, if they had tickets, her brothers took him with them. There was no hockey when he grew up in Florida, and he soon became an avid fan. When the kids started to arrive, every life event, from pee-wee football to junior high glee club to college graduations were fully attended by the entire clan and celebrated, sorrows and losses shared.

As a matter of fact, Josette's youngest brother had met a Tampa gal, Ida, at their wedding, one of Rick's cousins, and married her. They became the first family of snowbirds, summers in NY, winters in Florida. These connections brought both the families from different states closer together, for Rick and Josette, it let them stay close to ties at home. He knew he could not ask her to leave NY, to leave her family, even to raise a family of their own.

The first time they had flown back into NY, after their visit to Florida, he woke up just as they were circling the Statue of Liberty for their descent into JFK to find her crying quietly. He was surprised, she seemed so happy. He was concerned because his cousins in Tampa had not been nice. They kept comparing her to all the beautiful Latino girls he had dated. They said he was so handsome, he could have had anyone. Yeah, he said, like the girl who was so beautiful her mother told her never to smile and cause wrinkles. She was a blast. He was angry when they said goodbye, but Josette had not noticed any of it. "Honey, whatever it is, I'm sorry..." he blathered. She wiped away her tears, " I cry for happiness", she said, in her South Pacific movie accent. " It's just, I love this city so much. It's so unique.

You see it in movies, it's something, but in person, it's magic. I do this every time I come home from anywhere. I'm just a goose." "But you're my goose." He answered with relief.

It was a wonderful life, even better than the movie. They had three fine sons, good loving men who grew up to marry lovely, smart and kind women and had loving families of their own. They had their Potterville times of course, betrayals, disappointments, losses. But it was all ok, because every night, no matter what happened. He slept in her arms.

Now he was, sitting in her room at Edward White Hospital, in Florida, 60 years later. Her surgery had gone well. Now it was a matter of recovery. Their age was the challenge. She wasn't eating and hardly sleeping. She tossed and turned, her once lush figure now so fragile. The doctor said he wanted her vitals to be a bit more vital before he released her. The doctor thought himself witty. Rick thought he was a boor. There had never been a woman as vital as his Josette, just because she was different now; this joker had no right to talk about her that off-hand way. But he kept his opinion to himself, because that was what she would want.

A young nurse came and tried to tuck the blankets around her. Without even waking up, she threw them off and started her restless tossing back and forth again. Her breathing was so ragged, it scared him. "Oh child, you have to calm down and get some rest. You can't get better until your body shuts down long enough to heal"

He was sitting in the reclining chair in the dark on the other side of the bed.

He startled the nurse by saying quietly, "Can you imagine what it's like to be married to the same person for six decades? The young woman, recently divorced, answered bitterly, "I certainly can't".

He looked over at her dear form on the bed and saw it all at once. Like they say it is when you're drowning, but instead of water he was filling up with love; how young they had been, how much they had shared. For the millionth time he thought of what would have happened if he had missed that subway car.

He looked at the young nurse. Lush and healthy herself, she would probably be shocked to know that they still made love. It was different from those wild acrobatic days of their youth, when they would wind together for hours and hours and just stop for food and sleep. It was so fond, so gentle now, yet the passion still

inflamed him, as it had done, year after
year, every time she touched him.

Finally he answered his own question.
"It is heaven on earth." The nurse left
without comment. He walked over to
the bed. "This is what I should have
done all along." He lay down beside
her. She moved over slowly to make
room for him and then eased back, to
curve her body into his. He felt the
tension leave as she breathed deeply,
evenly now. He put his arms around
her, and they slept

The Great Ass

It was a Monday, the first time he saw Elena.
That always struck him as funny, such an
ordinary day. For your whole life to change
on a Monday. Here's how it happened, two of
his guys from the county road department
had been talking about this incredible ass on
a girl at the lunch stop. Dan was their
supervisor, new, from another state, one so
deep in the middle of America, it sometimes
felt like another world. Here, he wanted to
be respected as their boss, but he admitted he
was lonely and wanted to make friends,
buddies like he left back home. However,
when he had to listen to them talk on and on
about this girl with their kind of vulgar
reverence, he couldn't help being
uncomfortable with that kind of talk. So
much so that, finally, he agreed to go with
them for a quick lunch, as much to shut them
up as anything.

The place was surprising, a real roadside café
in the middle of nowhere with a little dirt

parking lot but every space was packed with trucks and pickups. Always a good sign, Dan thought, proved the locals ate there. Inside, it had a homey feel, a real mom and pop with posters and brilliant colored rugs on the walls, fanciful little statues of animals along with authentic Latin folk art peeking out from improbable places in the tiny building. Towards the back was a small trading post kind of shop, with the usual daily life supplies of motor oil and detergent, up front there was a glass counter full of homemade pastries and tortillas. It smelled delicious, his mouth watered, not like most places around here that made him feel queasy, all that fried stuff. They took a couple of tables; Mick and big Eric played the big shots and ordered lunch for him, like he was their date or something.

She greeted them with a friendly hello as soon as they sat down. It appeared she ran the place, greeted, seated and served as well as worked the register. Yet her manner was chill, almost serene in the middle of the busy lunch rush. There was one other waitress and a cook behind the window to the kitchen. The other girl walked past, and went to put down her plates on the first table.

The hostess barked out an order in Spanish. The waitress quickly did a 360 and put the meal down on the opposite table. Both women laughed. 'Sit where you dare" she told him.

That was exactly the kind of boss he wished he could be! He didn't even speak Spanish but he knew she was confident, firm but fair.

She was very pretty; he had to admit that right off. She was petite, with dark hair and light eyes, pale clear skin. She looked about 19, he thought, from his wise old age of 24, with a real flush of health, like he hadn't seen in the girls around here; all either pasty looking or fake tanned. He had missed the girls back home who looked fresh faced just because they just spent so much time outside. His stomach did a flip as he looked at her. He was probably hungry. Had he skipped breakfast? He felt he had to maintain a position for the guy's amusement so when they looked for his reaction, he just shrugged his shoulders.

Mick just laughed and elbowed big Eric. They giggled like teenage boys instead of the county road workers, that they really were. "Pay attention," Mr. Dan the Man, and behold perfection."

Mick strolled up to the side counter and asked the girl for a pack of smokes. Dan noticed he was ordering a different brand than his usual poison, and he quickly realized why. The cigarettes were stacked almost to the ceiling. This brand was on a very tall top shelf, and the girl turned around and stood on a small stool then reached up on tiptoes to get to the desired pack.

Dan felt his mouth go dry. After a second his throat began to close, he felt like he was choking, then he realized his mouth was hanging open. He took a drink of water. He had never in his life seen anything like it. Her ass was so round and perfect, for a minute he thought it could not be real. It popped right out of her slender young body, like a masthead on a magnificent ship. Mick was right, for once, more than right, God, he felt light headed, and she had the most perfect behind he had ever seen in his life!

He was not normally an ass man. Give him long legs, blond hair and big boobs - typical cheerleader material and he enjoyed the magazine ride as much as any man. But this, she, was different. He felt like he was sweating. Dan shot a quick look at the guys to see if they were having the same reaction. They were just staring like mad men at the girl as she now traveled from table to counter, then as they shoveled in delicious food between leers. The jerks. He was having a hard time breathing. Do 24 year olds have heart attacks? Should he see a cardiologist? Would that be covered by insurance for someone his age? He suddenly hated every man in the room for just looking at her.

Her whole figure was lovely; he could see that now, as she bustled around, seeming in constant motion like a dancer. She had full and firm breasts, a slender waist, and her hips were slight so that her butt seemed to just jut out of nowhere. He had to admit it. Simply put, her rear end was impossibly beautiful. The expression 'junk in the trunk came to mind' but it did not do her justice. He waxed poetic as he stared; it had pertitude. The ass was pert and sassy, and his first mad impression was that it had a sort of expression, almost a kind of pout, unlike the warm smile of its owner.

She had on tight blue jeans that were filled to their limit, they seemed to cling, separate and lift each cheek. Her butt was so round that it caused a little pucker in the middle of the back of her jeans. He wanted to slide his hand ever so gently down that inviting space, to experience all the promised delights down there.

Unable to resist, he saw himself slowly slide one hand into the inviting space at the back of her jeans. Her skin was so soft, so silky. He could feel the soft down of the tiny hairs on her as his fingertips explored the roundness. As his hand slid deeper he could actually feel the lush curves of it...

"Did you like it, Dan?"

Her voice crashing into his reverie.

The food, did you like the food?

"The food, of course, yeah, the food. No, it's wonderful, really, so fresh and young, I mean, so homemade, not like my home, I'm from Minnesota, but well, I just was not feeling myself and, Dan, you called me Dan? "

Without another word she smiled at his shirt, of course, his name tag.

He felt a sharp needle like pain in his knee. What the hell? Damn, that had not bothered him since high school. She turned away. The pain subsided.

Mickey looked at him too quickly for Dan to hide his expression. Mick and Eric both grinned, knowing that the derriere had made the desired impression.

Dan felt a little unwell. He looked down and saw he had now finished his meal the same as the other two slobs had. He had no memory of eating, or of tasting anything. What was happening? He decided he would need a full checkup, something was very wrong. He had always been healthy as a horse his mother would say, not sick a day in his life. Never overnight in hospital since the day he was born. Or in love, the thought came crashing over him.

Was this scary earthquake, sick to his stomach, feeling love? No way. Not like this, a Monday in a truck stop, with a girl who had smiled at him and everyone else. But, she smiled at him, he remembered fondly. That made him feel a bit better as he and the guys drove back to work. They gave him Tums when he was so quiet. He made the excuse of the spicy food. He knew he would be back there tomorrow. He knew he would be back every day from now on. He would just have to call his doctors back home and get his records sent here

Sometimes I think in poetry.

Words and rhymes just come to me,

I place them on a page,

in such a way

they would never be.

It seems to explain so much,

Of things that are so hard to say

In any other way.

Seashell

Loneliness can come

When your not at all alone,

In a crowd

Or even when

Some person is just talking too loud.

It hits you like a wave,

Crashing, tumbling, roiling

on you soul's hard shore

Tiny shell like memories

Glittering in the sun

Of your own dreamed past.

Longing rolls along your body,

Sending shivers

Saturating your day.

As you wade in the surf

You may stumble on

A golden conch,

Lift it to your ear.

Listen hard,

The calming ocean roars

And voices whisper

Behind the sea

You can hear those words

So near, so dear

'Hello darlin' my mother says,

A friends laughs,

Clear as a bell.

It makes you smile

In spite of the blues

And you go from lonely,

To lucky

Remembering love.

Sara Rude

A poetess once said to me,

I used to write like you,

Before I got my master's degree

And learned the real how to.

It's not just words upon a page,

But from form and function finely made,

The entire history of the spoken word

Must be understood before one writes verse.

She had her point

This much is true

I am indeed no Maya Angelu,

A Mary perhaps but an Oliver no way,

She thinks my poems are silly,

And that's ok.

They might be trite

But this much is true,

It comes directly from me to you.

My tears, my dreams, my sleepless nights,

Glimmers of emotions on empty pages,

I bear my soul because it feels right

For this one moment that we share.

Her poetry might be pandemic perfection,

A libretto of structure

Assonance divine,

But one last image let me draw,

and Excuse me please for this is crass,

She would not recognize

An original thought,

If it bit her in her poetic ass!

Emerson

A child born in early pandemic days

New eyes to see this world.

His young mother sits by the window

Watching trimmers groom trees,

her precious boy on her knee.

Locked down for safety,

New parent fears now magnified.

With no friendly arms to assuage,

The Village beyond still waiting

To embrace this new One.

A single tear

Steals down her cheek

And crashes on the

Soft downy head.

She wipes this away

With tender lips

And kisses a tiny seashell ear,

Tapping on the glass

Showing him outside,

She whispers

Words sad yet brave,

Look Baby,

People.

Tribute

Every morning as I sip my tea,

A wave of sadness crashes over me.

Enuni, regret, angst, and longing,

For those all friends and family

I never see,

For the me

I wanted so much to be.

A deep slow breath

Then a small sip,

A nice earl gray

in a china cup

or perhaps some oolong today.

Think about the day ahead,

And ponder this

Can I face with it hope

Instead of dread?

Finding small moments of delight,

A child's laugh,

a bird in flight

I can go outside

and Look at the sky

The blue so real it hurts my eyes,

Now I hear crows brilliant cries,

Come out and play,

The trees say Hi!

Another sip

and the wisdom comes,

Mares, I tell me,

you may have your troubles,

But you my friend,

make a damn fine cuppa!

Some days...

Some days I just don't feel like myself

I walk and talk and eat and sleep

And no one can see

that it is not me.

The real me sits up on a shelf

Watching and judging like an

Insane elf

She goes through the motions

Does laundry, picks up poops.

She ignores the faces

I make of her in the mirror

She thinks all I am is a goof.

She stops me from reaching out,

Sending birthday greetings

Even from leaving the house.

So if you were not there

When I needed a hand,

Or could not call

When you knew I would fall,

It's ok, it's cool.

Believe me,

she and I and we

Understand!

Acknowledgments

I know most authors thank all those people who helped with the book, but we want to thank those people who helped us stick around to be able to write this book!

Compassion and kindness and caring about the details are the ineffable qualities that make the difference between life and death when your health is on the line. These people gave us all that and more, hope for a future: Dr. Christopher Koebbe, Chris, Dr Matthew Irvin, Stephanie, Jane Elson, LCSW,BCD,

Dr. Michael DiDonno, Dr Thomax Mixa, Carol Streigt.

A special thanks to the Pinellas County Office of Human Rights; Frank, Linda and Alana. Thank you for treating us like humans and getting us a home where we were physically able to write this book and enjoy our lives.

Thank you to Kylie McGivern, for always listening with an open heart and sharing the true stories.

Claudia Wolfe, you have helped Richard and I from the start of this strange brain trip. You shared your knowledge of what heals and the wisdom of your loving heart. Like the coffee pot Dick bought us as a wedding present 37 years ago, every single day you have helped us fill that cup of joy!

 John Marsh was our beloved Editor on several stories and a vital source of support and friendship, then, now and forever.

We also want to thank Richard's sister Celeste and bros Bobby and Danny, for all the great phone calls.

Thanks to Belicia, Robin, Tiffany, John, Greg, Jimmy and Craig for coming personally in person to visit after Richard's brain surgery. The interaction with friends has been more than motivating; it is essential to build new neural pathways, to give Richard's brain a new life! Thank you, thank you.

The best I save for last, Jennifer and Steve, thank you for Emerson.

ABOUT THE AUTHORS

Mary Ellen & Richard DiPietra

The DiPietra's began their collaboration with cohabitation in Hell's Kitchen, NYC in 1981. 37 years of marriage later, they have co-produced; one amazing son, two plays (I am a Cuban Sandwich and The Ybor Stories) and one book(I am a Cuban Sandwich).

In March 2022 Richard underwent brain
stent surgery. At 73, with a little help from
his friends, he is on the mend.
To regain ability he uses music, dancing,
singing and puzzles. Writing has been a
powerful tool in regaining cognitive function.
This is their second book.

Look for the audio book of IAACS read by
Richard out this spring on Amazon Audible.

Where to buy the book?

Amazon.com

Please pretty please with sugar on top
share reviews on our books on good
reads, amazon, google! Will swap
reviews for reviews!

Check out our first book and the perfect companion...

I Am A Cuban Sandwich

All This and A Bag of Chips

All This and A Bag of Chips

All This and A Bag of Chips

All This and A Bag of Chips

All This and A Bag of Chips

All This and A Bag of Chips

All This and A Bag of Chips

.

All This and A Bag of Chips

All This and A Bag of Chips

All This and A Bag of Chips

All This and A Bag of Chips

All This and A Bag of Chips

All This and A Bag of Chips

Made in the USA
Las Vegas, NV
15 January 2023

65661617R00059